HAVING EVERYTHING

A NOVEL

BY JEANNE GALE

Cover art by Michelle Murphy-Ferguson
michellemferguson27@gmail.com

Cover and interior layout by Clark Kenyon

ISBN: 978-1-7322986-1-3

Library of Congress Control Number: 2019907923

Disclaimer: Although *Having Everything* was inspired by true events, the names, characters, places and events are recreated through the author's imagination or are used fictitiously. Any resemblance to actual persons, living or dead, businesses, companies, events, or locales, is entirely coincidental.

Published by Jeanne Gale jeannegale8@gmail.com

Accolades

With infinite gratitude:

I thank my sisters, Katherine Margua Simon and Rura Ann Griffith, for loving me and my stories and challenging me, always.

Thank you, Charles (Charlie) Carlisle, my dear brilliant friend who patiently edited, nudged and prodded me to let go of all my darlings in favor of the story.

And, to my extraordinary writers' group, John Daniels, Nancy Wheeler, Dave Mohrmann, Wanda Naylor and Pete Springer, The Great Intenders, thank you.

I could never have done this without all of you.

Cover artist: Michelle Murphy-Ferguson. Thank you, Michelle. Our collaboration was a great success.

Author's Foreword

I was a young lawyer working in California when the judge appointed me to defend Artemesia in juvenile court. I'm not young anymore and my memories have woven a tapestry of her that has colored and ripened with time. Yet, even after all these years, I cannot forget what happened nor can I forgive myself for my failure to anticipate the depth of human cruelty.

My client lived with her father and her four younger siblings at a migrant farm in California. I was acquainted with the culture of migrant camps as I occasionally accompanied my father in his journeys to attend to the health, welfare and education of migrating people and native American people in California and other western states. The federal agency that oversaw these matters was my father's employer.

I had also become acquainted with immigrants

from Mexico though my father's friend, Bonifacio, his wife, Artemesia, their children, and extended family. They were our neighbors for two years while my father attended a university. When our house burned down, Bonifacio, Artemesia, and their family took us in. I have borrowed their names for this story out of my love for them and my desire to protect, as much as is still possible, the young woman I represented in juvenile court.

Artemesia's humanity touched my soul. Her story taught me to embrace laughter and passion and unconditional love because sometimes that's all you have.

I hope you see her in the people you meet in your life.

With Love,

Jeanne Gale

HAVING EVERYTHING

"Stranger coming fast," Artemesia called.

Before the truck reached them, the children disappeared into the grape vines. The sound of their shoes thumping in the soft dirt was masked by the truck's roaring engine. Haidee was in front when she raised her hand to stop them. Peering through the leaves they watched their father and Mr. Markilsen walk toward the truck.

"You thieving sons-of-bitches!" the man in the truck screamed over the engine noise. "You stole seven families from my camp!"

"Settle down, Trouckman," Mr. Markilsen said. "They'd already left your camp when they came to Garcia for work. You know that."

"Garcia bribed them," Trouckman said, jabbing his

finger out of the truck window toward Papa. "They'd a never left my camp if he didn't promise 'em more money."

"He agreed to pay them what we pay all the migrants, Trouckman," Mr. Markilsen said. "If you weren't holding back part of their pay for camp fees and garden space, you'd have enough workers for harvest."

"Keep that spic foreman of yours away from my workers!" Trouckman spit out his words. "Wrong you hired Garcia, he's illegal," he said, still poking his finger at Papa. "Should'a hired a local boy like my Jerry." Clouds of angry gray dust billowed behind the truck as he drove away.

"I'm sorry hiring those workers caused a problem, sir," Papa said.

"This isn't your fault, Bonifacio," Mr. Markilsen said, "Those families were headed to Modesto if you hadn't hired them. Your girl, Artemesia, told me. Trouckman's a hot head."

"Thank you, sir," Papa said. "I should get back to work."

"That's enough for today," Mr. Markilsen said. "Spend some time with your kids."

"I've got a pitcher of limeade and ice," Papa said. "Will you stay for a glass?"

"Don't mind if I do, Bonifacio."

Their father purposefully nodded toward the place they were hiding. Artemesia, Haidee, Maria, Julio and Lucinda walked slowly from behind the grape vines. Their faces wore worry. Lucinda, clutching Artemesia's hand, was in front as they joined their father who stood near Mr. Markilsen.

"Hello, Sir," Artemesia said.

The younger children put on their practiced

pleasant faces and looked toward Mr. Markilsen, but did not speak, then looked at Papa.

Glancing across the clearing toward home, Papa said, "Bring out the limeade and ice for everyone. Then get your homework started."

As the children hurried toward their house, Maria asked, "Artemesia, will that man with the truck come back?

"I don't know," Artemesia answered. "But, if he does, remember the rule, go into the vineyard and watch until Papa or I nod for you come out. Let's go inside. You can help Lucinda with the ice."

Heidee lifted the good pitcher from the top shelf while Lucinda and Maria wrestled a block of ice from the chest next to the back wall. Artemesia pulled the jar of limeade from the cupboard and Julio danced around the kitchen with the ice pick.

"Julio, what are you doing?" Artemesia asked.

"Dancing," he said. He was wearing his brown cowboy boots with "Julio" tooled into the leather. The boots had been his birthday present, along with Papa's lesson in leather tooling. He wore them all the time. Julio spun on his heel, jabbing the ice pick higher as he stamped his other foot. "I don't have homework. Let's turn on the radio and dance."

"Stop it," Artemesia said. "That's dangerous." She took the ice pick from his hand and put it on the counter.

"You can't always do what you want." Haidee said, frowning at her brother. "Papa won't like us to play music while Mr. Markilsen's here. We all work for him. That's what Papa said. We wouldn't have a place to live without him."

"Julio, it's Wednesday," Artemesia said. "We can dance after we finish our homework and after Mr. Markilsen goes home. Anyway, Papa won't let you

5

turn on the radio while we have company or until all of us finish our homework. Not just you."

"But we can't dance tomorrow, and Mr. Markilsen might stay a long time," Julio said. "Then, Papa won't dance with me."

There was no time on Tuesdays or Thursdays, for family dancing in the evening. Two years ago, when Artemesia was a high school sophomore, she started teaching English to two other migrants at their camp.

Mrs. Carrera and her son, Jorge. Artemesia remembered how nervous they seemed when they asked her for English lessons. Then, as time passed, more people asked to come to her class. Papa had learned English as a boy, working with his parents at a migrant camp. The foreman's wife had taught him. *I'm passing the gift forward*, she thought. She knew learning English meant more job possibilities for a migrant, and a better opportunity to obtain a green card, even a chance for citizenship. Papa only allowed classes on Tuesdays and Thursdays. He said the other days were for family. It wasn't long before Haidee, Maria, and Julio were teaching English classes with Artemesia. Even Lucinda helped Maria and Julio teach the youngest children. But tonight, it was Wednesday, a dancing night.

Mr. Markilsen and Papa sat on one side of the outside table talking softly and sipping their sweet bitter iced drinks. Drips of condensation slid from their glasses over their leathery hands and made tiny splashes on the table. The air was the kind of warm that was hot, unless you'd felt the midday heat, then it was almost cool.

Homework occupied Artemesia and her sisters, Haidee and Maria, on the side of the table furthest from Papa and Mr. Markilsen. Lucinda sat next to

Artemesia with Julio, who drew tic-tac-toe boxes, winning each game against his youngest sister.

Finally, Mr. Markilsen stood up and Papa followed. He shook Papa's hand and said, "Don't worry about Trouckman, Bonifacio. Goodbye children."

Artemesia and the younger children also stood. "Goodbye sir," Artemesia said. They returned his wave, watching as he walked toward the parking area.

"Papa, I don't have any homework," Julio said, as soon as Mr. Markilsen was a good distance away. "Let's turn on the radio."

"We do too have homework," Maria said. "Mrs. Fredrickson told us to write an essay on our five favorite things to do." She pinched her lips together and scowled at her twin brother.

"She doesn't expect us to finish it tonight," Julio said.

"Begin your essay, Julio," Papa said. "No radio until everyone else finishes their homework."

With no air-conditioning in the house and only small spaces to work, homework was always done at the outside table Papa had built, unless it was raining. When Mr. Markilsen had ordered a shed be torn down, Papa asked for the left-over boards. After he nailed three, two-by-fours across five of the long boards, they all helped lift the new tabletop onto the reinforced sawhorses. That big table became the center of their outdoor living space. The benches Papa built were moved around from the table to the fire pit. Strings of lights extended from the house and around the outside living area on boards mounted across the top of fence posts.

Haidee was the last one to finish her homework. "Julio," she called. "Go turn on the radio."

After a few minutes, Julio tugged Artemesia's shirt,

distracting her from the beat of the Salsa music and the chopped salad she was preparing. "Papa's not dancing with me," he said.

Papa was sitting at the table with his eyes open, but he wasn't seeing. It felt like he was looking inside himself. Artemesia knew that her father loved the rhythms of Salsa. He would usually stand by the fire pit with Julio, clapping and stomping in the soft dirt and singing.

"Papa, why aren't you dancing?" Artemesia asked.

"Mr. Trouckman's temper today worried me," Papa said.

Artemesia dried her hands and sat down next to her father. "Mr. Markilsen said you didn't do anything wrong," she said.

"I know," Papa said. "I told Mr. Markilsen about the last time Mr. Trouckman was angry with me, but I never told you and I should have. It was a couple years ago, after I went to Mexico to search for Mama. Mr. Trouckman's foreman, Jerry Blankden, called my cellphone and said he was on the Mexico side, near the border crossing. He asked if I wanted a ride back to our camp. He told me he'd just brought their migrant workers back to Mexico, after harvest."

"I never knew he offered you a ride," Artemesia said. "That was a good thing, right?"

"I thought so too. After Jerry picked me up, he told me Mr. Trouckman was angry about Mr. Markilsen making me foreman, and even more angry that we picked our crops before they did. But then he said Mr. Trouckman was angry with everyone, even Jerry, because our grapes reached the market before theirs. Since Jerry said his Boss was mad at both of us, it never occurred to me he would start a fight. I ended up hitting Jerry."

"You hit Mr. Blankden?"

"Yes, and I shouldn't have," Papa said. "When we got to the border crossing, the guards asked us to get out of the passenger van. While the guard was looking at Jerry's passport and my green card, Jerry hit me in the stomach. Then, he started yelling that I attacked him. He took another run at me, swinging his fists and yelling, so I blocked him and hit him in the face. It was stupid of me to take the bait. The border police believed I had attacked Jerry, or they just said that because he's a citizen. They took my green card."

"You never told me," Artemesia said. "Papa, this is important. That's why Mr. Trouckman called you illegal, isn't it?"

"Probably," Papa said. "I just told Mr. Markilsen about it. After what happened today at the clearing, I thought he should know.

"But, Papa. If you don't have a green card, we're all illegal."

"I know, it's not good. But you didn't enter the Unites States illegally, only me. But I should have told you a long time ago. Mama and I planned for our children to become citizens when each of you turn eighteen. And, since you never entered illegally, you can still do that."

"But Papa, if you had told me we could have tried to get your green card back. Mr. Markilsen would have helped you."

"I don't know how anyone could help me get my green card back." Papa said. "The Border Guard believed I had started the fight. When he took my green card, he entered my number into the computer and told me I was not allowed to enter the United States. If Jerry Blankden or his boss, Mr. Trouckman, told immigration that Jerry lied, maybe I could get it back. But that is never going to happen."

Papa stopped talking and looked down at his hands for a minute, then continued, "But, most of all I was ashamed that I couldn't find Mama. The green card didn't seem important. Mr. Markilsen told me the farm bureau has an agreement with immigration that migrant camps are off limits. It's necessary if they want the crops harvested. Most of the migrant workers don't have a green card."

Artemesia's mind plunged into problem solving as she nodded. After Papa became foreman, they lived at the camp all year, no longer crossing the border for harvest. But unless they figured out how to get Papa's green card back, he couldn't apply for citizenship. Mama would have had an idea. She remembered one year, long ago, a few weeks before they were to return to Mexico after the harvest was finished.

She and Mama were helping Mrs. Markilsen in her vegetable garden.

"This garden is too much for me and my husband to manage," Mrs. Markilsen had said. "There is too much work here at the ranch after you leave."

To which, Mama had replied, "Maybe Bonifacio and the children and I could help more if we stayed all year."

A week later, Mr. Markilsen had asked Papa to stay all year and promoted him to foreman.

Artemesia's heart ached for her mother's touch, to have her strong arms squeeze her too tight one more time. Lucinda didn't remember Mama very well. She was six when Mama left. Maria and Julio, who were eighteen months older, were sad, but somehow the twins seemed able to console each other. But for Artemesia and Haidee, like Papa, losing Mama broke their hearts. Sometimes it felt like she was here only a moment ago, but she had been gone three years.

Artemesia had never told anyone about the mind-conversations she had with her mother. She presented her dilemma and stopped being frightened about things she couldn't change. Her mother's warmth seemed to guide her to solutions and understanding. *There are so many people from Mexico who apply for a green card,* she thought, *and they're denied, even though they have never broken the law. How could we get Papa a new green card when he came across the border illegally?* She knew the answer as soon as the question formed in her mind. Sorrow, no stranger to Artemesia, crept in as her heart sunk deep with the understanding. *We can't.*

***

The next morning Artemesia, Haidee, Julio, Maria and Lucinda stood at the edge of the vineyard watching the heat-shimmer tremble from the approaching school bus. When the bus stopped and the door opened, Haidee, Julio, Maria and Lucinda all went to the back. The grammar school was at the end of the route. High school students were required to sit in the front half of the bus, no exceptions.

Artemesia climbed into the bus last. She walked past Danny Blankden, who sat alone two rows back from the door, and then Bea Ledderton and Janet Stewart, who sat together behind Danny. Artemesia sat alone, five rows behind the driver, and looked out the window at the vineyard. No one ever sat with her. No one had ever invited her to sit with them. Artemesia was used to that. For three years they had been on the bus before her and they had never spoken to her. Two stops later, Jimmy Trouckman and Lloyd

17

Decker got on the bus. Like always, Lloyd pulled Bea to her feet and slid in next to his girlfriend, Janet. Jimmy sat in front of them with Danny, and Bea squeezed in between the two boys.

When the bus stopped at the high school, she was, as always, the last to exit. Julio tapped on the bus window as Artemesia walked by. She looked up to see her brother and sisters watching her. She waved before the bus pulled away, then walked toward her homeroom class. It was almost three weeks into her senior year of high school.

This was her last year of school. Artemesia hadn't told Papa that college wasn't possible anymore, since their family wasn't legal. She had filled out the registration paperwork with Mama before she entered high school. The form required you state your citizenship and green card number. She had registered as a migrant worker's child under Papa's green card.

Mama and Papa had been clear that learning was Artemesia's first job. "The teacher has the job of teaching, but even more important, the student has the job of learning," Mama had said. "Be curious, don't waste any opportunity to learn." When students grumbled about assignments, Artemesia never joined in that sentiment, even inside. She remembered watching her father when Mr. Markilsen asked him to do a job, she didn't think was possible. "Yes, Sir," Papa would say, "I'll do my best." Sometimes he couldn't do the job perfectly, or all in one day, but he always tried. And Mr. Markilsen seemed happy with Papa's effort. *Without school, I'll need a different job next year*, Artemesia thought.

Artemesia reached her classroom and sat in her usual front row seat.

"Good morning," Mrs. Taylor said to the class. "Your next project is to complete a college application.

These are specific for Fresno State University, but other universities have similar requirements. Arti, will you pass these out?" She handed Artemesia a stack of the applications. "I expect everyone to put their best effort into this project. Whether you pursue college or employment, this exercise will help you prepare for after high school."

Mrs. Taylor had been Artemesia's home room teacher since she started high school. On the first day's roll call she told Artemesia that she had given her the nickname of "Arti," and entered it in the school computer for the other teachers. Artemesia had wondered why Jedediah didn't have his name shortened. His name had as many syllables as her name. But she didn't say anything.

The students had been working quietly for fifteen minutes when Mrs. Turner interrupted, "Mr.

Blankden, is there a reason you've stopped working on the project?"

"Yeah," Danny said. "This is all crap."

"Watch your language," Mrs. Taylor said.

"I'm not going to college," Danny said.

"In any job, following instructions is important," Mrs. Taylor said. "If you ever choose a different path, this project will help you define your abilities and interests."

"I already know my job," Danny said. "I'm gonna work for Mr. Trouckman, be his next foreman, just like my old man. It's all worked out."

"Danny, you are required to complete this assignment to have credit for my class," Mrs. Taylor said.

Artemesia watched Jimmy Trouckman look toward her then gesture behind his book with his middle finger. Danny nodded. Danny had been in Artemesia's homeroom and ridden the same bus since

21

they started high school. She wondered if Danny would turn out like his father, Jerry Blankden. The man who'd tricked Papa into fighting. She'd never thought of Danny as a bad person, just someone who didn't care about school, someone who looked up to people with power and money, especially Jimmy Trouckman's family, more than education.

"Oh, you want me to be like Arti," Danny whined. "Be perfect, finish every project, suck-up and follow the rules."

Artemesia quietly winced. She tried to be unseen at school, but Mrs. Taylor had arthritis and could barely walk. In the beginning of the school year, she had volunteered to pass out papers and collect things when needed. She'd never thought of it as a way to get something from Mrs. Taylor.

"Danny!" Mrs. Taylor said. "Do you really want to

spend the rest of your senior year in the principal's office?

The classroom door opened and Mr. Ellsworth, the vice-principal, asked Mrs. Taylor if he could speak to her a moment.

Mrs. Taylor stood up slowly and turned to Danny. "Complete your college application assignment or expect a long detention," she said, before hobbling out of the classroom.

Jimmy Trouckman, sitting next to Danny, snickered and whispered loud enough for the class to hear, "Hey, man, it's just a stupid exercise. Anyway, Mexican migrant brats don't go to college. Her spic father's an illegal. College isn't going to happen for her, man."

Janet Stewart looked down at her desk and Bea Ledderton glared at Artemesia. Mrs. Taylor walked back into the classroom and smiled at Danny as he turned his application over and picked up his pen.

It's a big deal for a migrant girl to finish high school, Artemesia thought. *I know I can't go to college now and Papa won't be too disappointed. With Mama gone, he'll need me to help.*

But it hurt Artemesia to let go of the idea of college. Her studies had been her priority for so long. Ending her education before college hadn't quite sunk in until Jimmy's comment. But, as soon as Papa told her he was illegal, she'd known. She loved learning new things, especially math, discovering shapes and movement in the numeric formulas. Mr. Simpson had given her one of the Einstein impossibility puzzles and he was excited when she figured out why it couldn't be solved. It needed one more number, which she determined could be only one of three choices. He had written an article about the puzzle solution and added her name as his student researcher. Her teachers all assumed she would go to college, but none of them were migrants.

She found the citizenship question on the third page. A real college application would reveal her father's illegal status. The whole family would be deported. College was no longer possible. She left the category blank and moved to the next question. Artemesia worked meticulously on the application until the bell rang for her next class.

After school, Artemesia nodded to her sisters and brother sitting in the back row of the bus. Taking her regular seat, she looked out the bus window and wondered how to explain to Papa that she wouldn't attend college. Before Mr. Markilsen asked Papa to be the foreman, Papa had worked fourteen-hour days every harvest for six years. That was four years ago. Now they lived at the camp all year and attended school. Even though college had been part of Mama and Papa's plan for her, with Mama gone and Papa without a green card, everything was different. College isn't a big deal, she kept telling herself. But she knew it was a lie.

***

Papa was standing outside the house when they got home. "Okay my children, I've got to get back to work. You all have homework. And be sure to start the stew before the English class," he said.

After they finished their homework, Maria and Lucinda brought the English teaching books outside to the table. Artemesia filled a large pot about one-quarter full of water and carried it to the outdoor propane stove. Julio and Haidee cut up a chicken and chopped garlic and celery on the sink counter inside. After they put everything into the stainless-steel bowl, Julio carried it outside, stood on his tiptoes, and tipped the contents into the pot. Haidee added salt and the fresh rosemary Artemesia had picked from their garden.

Julio, Lucinda and Maria chased each other and played hide and seek while Artemesia and Haidee washed Papa's work clothes and hung them on the lines. Julio, covered with dust, ran up to Artemesia. "I'm hungry, he said."

"Get away from Papa's clean clothes," Haidee said. "They're still wet. Did you roll in the dirt?"

Lucinda ran up next to Julio. "He tripped and pretended he did it on purpose," she said. "Then, he rolled in the dirt. A lot. I told you you'd get in trouble."

"Julio," Artemesia said. "Go change clothes and put the dirty ones in the basket. I'm hungry too. How about a bean and cheese tortilla before the others get here?"

Julio dashed into the house. Everyone followed. Lucinda took the lid from the tortilla container on the counter. Artemesia grated cheese from the block. Haidee scooped two spoonfuls of beans into the tortillas as her sisters held them open. Julio formed the end of the line holding his tortilla open with his dirt caked hands.

"I have clean clothes," he said, in response to Haidee's frowning inspection.

"I see that," she said. "but your hands and face still have dirt. Go wash. I'll fill your tortilla and put it on the counter for you.

Twenty minutes later, Papa arrived before the students. "Smells good."

"Yes," Artemesia said. "We each had a bean and cheese tortilla. Do you want one?"

"Not yet," he said. "I'll have tortillas with my stew. "How's homework going?"

"I wrote my essay," Julio said. "Haidee checked my spelling this time."

"Good work, Julio," Papa said. "You too, Haidee."

"I'm getting ready for when Artemesia goes to college," Haidee said. "I'll be the oldest kid at home."

"That's true," Papa said, "Next year Artemesia will be in college and in five years, it will be your turn, Haidee."

"I'm not going to college," Artemesia said. "You need me here, helping out, and anyway, migrants can't go to college."

"Oh yes they can, and you are!" Papa said. "That's not negotiable young lady. Your sisters and brother are managing fine. We'll even continue the English classes now that you have everyone in the family teaching. We need to start your college application."

Slowly, he lowered his angular jaw as he looked at Artemesia. His dark eyes seemed to bore into her as she studied his face. It was his immoveable look. Nothing she could say would change his mind.

"Okay, Papa," she said.

She couldn't bring herself to remind him they were all illegal, or even tell him about Jimmy Trouckman's comment. It would do no good to argue that losing his green card changed her eligibility. Papa believed his children were entitled to attend college because they hadn't personally broken the law. But she knew in her heart Jimmy was right about one thing; illegal migrant kids don't go to college.

"We're filling out sample college applications as an exercise in my homeroom," Artemesia said.

"Good," Papa said. "You have experience. Use the school computer to research scholarships and application requirements and you and I will work on this together. Let's have an agreement to complete the application and mail it in three weeks."

"Hi, Mr. Ortega, Jose," Maria said, as her student arrived with his father and two carrots. Within a few minutes the rest of the eleven students had added their vegetables to the chicken stew. Limeade, glasses and a stack of tortillas were already on the table when they arrived. While the vegetables cooked, Artemesia sorted everyone by reading level and assigned her sisters and brother to lead the different groups. Fifteen minutes later everyone was eating chicken vegetable stew with tortillas and practicing their English lesson.

The next three weeks were long and slow for Artemesia, between school, homework, chores, English classes at the camp, and the college application. She would have never finished the application without Papa's help. The family information, particularly where they had lived before the Markilsen camp, seemed like a blur. Then writing essays on different topics, gathering letters in support of admission, and preparing a separate scholarship application with essays and letters in support left no spaces in her days. But the hardest part for Artemesia was knowing that this was nothing more than an exercise. Every word she wrote for the application cut "*you can't go to college*" a little deeper into her heart.

"Okay, Papa," Artemesia said. "It's done. I finished the supporting letter requests and gave one to each of my teachers, as well as Mr. Johnston and Mr. Markilsen. The essays and the application were proofread by you, Haidee and Mrs. Taylor. The only missing item is a letter from a family member. You're my only adult family member. Here's the packet and you get to mail it."

"*Excelente*," Papa said. "And I've already written my letter. Since the supporting letters go directly to admissions and not through the applicant, I didn't tell you."

"May I read it?" Artemesia said.

"No," Papa said. "Not yet."

The hopefulness in her father's face felt terrible to Artemesia as she bore the certainty of his disappointment.

***

Two months later, Artemesia was in her chemistry class when she received a note to meet with the principal.

"Hello, Mr. Johnston," she said. "Did you ask to see me?" She stood in front of his massive desk with her hands clasped.

"Yes," he said. "I have good news for you. You have been accepted at Fresno State University with a full scholarship. Your tuition, dormitory, meals and books will be paid for. Assuming you keep your scholastic status through graduation."

"Oh my. They let me go to college?" Artemesia said. "I'm a migrant. We..., I mean, well, my father..." Artemesia looked down and gathered her courage. "Mr. Johnston, my father no longer has a green card. He is not in the country legally."

"Arti, your father already told me that. You had left the citizenship box unchecked in the application. The University contacted me regarding the omission, and I called your father. He arranged for Mr. Markilsen to act as your legal guardian."

Artemesia felt her heart jump into her throat. She couldn't speak, she could barely breathe as she collapsed into the chair next to Mr. Johnston's desk. Her cheeks felt hot as teardrops slid down her face. She sniffed, trying to regain her composure.

Mr. Johnston smiled and held up the Kleenex box.

"There now," he said. "You will do well in college. Your grade point average alone qualified you for your scholarship, but I believe your father's letter about your character was a large factor in securing your full scholarship. I made you a copy."

"Thank you, sir," she said. Her hand trembled as she took the letter. She looked up to see a warm smile on Mr. Johnston's face. *College… for me.*

***

Artemesia waited at the school bus stop. She had folded Papa's letter into her journal. One of the reasons Papa was the foreman was because he spoke and wrote both English and Spanish. He loved to read, and he could handle any paperwork in either language. She had read his words so many times that one passage locked in her memory and in her heart.

"… and I watched as Artemesia held Lucinda, after

I had lost hope. I listened to her story of her mother stirring a pot and singing. We had nothing. I had fallen into such grief I could not climb out. But Artemesia's words moved the spoon as she sang my wife's song to the rhythm of the stirring, and my eyes cleared. My daughter sees life's joy in hidden places. Beyond her scholastic accomplishments, please see my daughter. She is our best hope and maybe yours too. ...."

Just thinking about his words took her breath away. She smiled. Papa wouldn't like her to lie to herself. So, maybe, his letter was about who she dreamed of being, someday.

Artemesia climbed into the school bus, waved at her sisters and brother, and sat where she always sat. Jimmy Trouckman and his friends were the last to arrive before the bus driver pulled away from the curb. *I was so sure Jimmy was right. That I would never go to college. Everything is different now. Maybe it's good they don't know.* She held her smile inside.

***

Walking home from the bus stop, Haidee walked backwards watching Artemesia.

"What?" she said.

"Are you trying to read my mind?" Artemesia asked.

"Yes! What's up with you?" Haidee replied.

"Okay, I'll tell you. I have a scholarship to college."

"I knew you would get a scholarship," Haidee said. "You're the smartest one."

"I'm just older," Artemesia said. "Each of us have something we're really good at."

"Will you come home after school, like now?" Lucinda asked.

"She has to live at her school for college." Julio said.

"How far away is the college?" Maria asked.

"It's too far to come home every day. The college has a dormitory for students," Artemesia said. "I guess I'll live there and come home during summer and holidays, and whenever I can."

"What will you study?" Haidee asked.

"I don't know."

When they reached the house, Papa was standing outside. Haidee, Julio, Maria, and Lucinda ran across the clearing squealing Artemesia's news. Artemesia walked into her father's open arms. Grinning, he leaned down and kissed her cheek.

"Good," was all he said before his usual Tuesday afterschool speech, "Get the stew started and finish your homework before the English class starts. I'll be back at seven."

***

On Friday, after homeroom, assembly was held in the gymnasium. Artemesia and her lab partner, Sharon, sat together in the bleachers. They first met when they were sophomores. Sharon asked Artemesia to write out her full name and pronounce it, and Sharon had never forgotten.

The secretary voice crackled from the overhead speakers as she read a list of club events, then announced that one of the history teachers was retiring, somebody had graffitied the boy's bathroom, again, and students with cars couldn't park in the west lot next week because they were painting stripes. When she finished, Mr. Johnston came to the podium.

"Ladies and gentlemen, today we honor those senior students who have received college scholarships. When I call your name, please come and stand on the stage with me."

He began calling the names alphabetically. "Charlene Adams, Jeremiah Abernathy, Leroy Brellsome, Jennifer Freidman, …. Arti Garcia…"

"Get up, Artemesia," Sharon said, shoving her from the bleacher. "You have to go down there. Go on."

Artemesia's knees nearly buckled as she stood up. The gymnasium filled with applause, just as it had for every student named before her. They were clapping, and students called out their congratulations as she passed.

After everyone was on the stage, Mr. Johnson said, "Let's give our scholarship students another round of applause for their hard work."

Mr. Johnson excused everyone twenty minutes before their next class. Sharon appeared next to Artemesia and put her arm around her.

A tear slid down Artemesia's cheek.

"Come on girlfriend," Sharon said. "I'm buying you a Coke."

After they walked to the tables next to the concession machines, Sharon fed the machine two dollars and brought back their drinks.

"Are you all right?" Sharon asked. "You looked like you were going to faint."

"I felt like it, too," Artemesia said. "Being called up to the stage."

"In addition to you being the smartest person at the school, you're also the shyest," Sharon said.

"People clapped for me," Artemesia said.

"Of course they clapped," Sharon said. "Did you think everyone was as big a jerk as Jimmy Trouckman and his thuggy friends?"

"Well, not you," Artemesia said.

"You need to meet more people," Sharon said. "I didn't apply for a scholarship because my grades weren't good enough. I'm lucky my parents agreed to pay my tuition."

Everything changed so fast. Artemesia had been so sure she would never attend college, and now ….

**

On Monday, Sharon and Artemesia were eating lunch in the high-school cafeteria and speculating about college when Jimmy Trouckman walked by with his usual group. They were bunched together whispering and stared briefly at Artemesia, together. Lloyd and Janet stood out in the group as they looked particularly unhappy. Then, quickly, they all looked away. She thought about what Sharon had called them. *Thuggy friends…. I never thought of them that way.*

After lunch, Sharon and Artemesia walked in different directions. Three more classes before the end of the school day. Artemesia had to force her mind back to her studies. She concentrated... English Literature was her next class. She had already given her report, but she would be scoring and commenting with the rest of the class on the remaining students' reports.

Heading home on the bus, she waved at her family and sat in her usual seat. Jimmy Trouckman and his friends got on together. They all smiled at Artemesia. Then Bea came right up to her row and sat next to her.

"Hi, Arti," Bea said. "Congratulations on your scholarship. Last Friday, when Mr. Johnston called you to the stage, it really inspired us; Jimmy, in particular. Look." Bea pointed to Jimmy who was nodding and smiling at her. "So, we're having a party at Jimmy's house next Saturday. A bunch of kids from school are coming and we'll have music and swimming. He has a pool. Jimmy's inviting the older kids from his Dad's migrant camp too. We all want you to come. To get to know you better. How about it?"

Artemesia just stared at her, trying to wrap her mind around the words. Finally, she spoke, "Bea, what's this really about? You've never spoken to me before."

"We all talked after the assembly. After Mr. Johnston said you have a scholarship to college," Bea said. "The truth is, we don't know you. We saw you as a migrant, not one of us."

"I am a migrant," Artemesia said. "If my father's job ends, we go back to Mexico."

"Everybody knows your father's job won't end," Bea said. "Markilsen needs him, Jimmy's dad even said that."

Mr. Trouckman knows you're inviting me?" Artemesia asked.

"Yeah," Bea said. "We all talked it over together on the weekend, I mean about your scholarship and everything. Mr. Trouckman, Jimmy and me, Danny and his dad, Lloyd and Janet, we were all there."

Artemesia looked at Bea, then over at Jimmy and Danny. They were nodding and smiling. Janet's words, *you need to meet more people*, ran through her mind. But, how could she trust them?

"You know that Danny's father got my father's green card taken by the border guards, right?" Artemesia asked.

"Um, well," Bea said. She looked over at Jimmy.

Jimmy stood up and walked into the isle next to Bea.

"We talked about that too," Jimmy said. "We need to make that right. My father said we could talk to immigration and tell them it was a big misunderstanding at the border. See if we could get his green card back. You can talk to him more about that at the party."

Artemesia couldn't refuse now, not with the possibility of getting Papa's green card back. Everything, the whole family plan of citizenship could go back on track.

"If I came to this party," Artemesia said, "your father would really help get my father's green card back?

"Absolutely," Jimmy said, as he turned and walked back to his seat.

"And, you'd invite the migrants from Mr. Trouckman's camp? Artemesia asked.

"Oh sure," Bea answered. "I told you, that's the plan."

"May I invite Mr. Trouckman's migrant workers to my English class?"

Bea squirmed and looked at Jimmy. He nodded.

"Okay," Bea said. "It's a deal."

"Not a deal," Artemesia said. "I still need to ask

my father and Jimmy needs to ask his father about his workers attending my class."

"Great," Bea said. "I'm sure everyone will agree. Do you have a bathing suit for swimming?"

"Uh, no," Artemesia said.

"Don't worry," Bea said, "I'll bring an extra for you."

***

Artemesia was still mulling over the strange invitation during supper. She was glad it was the twins' night to wash the dishes.

"Will you walk with me?" Artemesia asked Papa.

That was the house code for, *I want to talk*. Their house, although the biggest of the migrant camp houses, was only three hundred square feet and offered no space for private conversations.

It had cooled to the low eighties as Artemesia

pressed her bare feet into the soft dirt while she followed Papa to the outside table.

After they sat down Papa asked, "Is this about going to college?"

"Not directly, but related," Artemesia said. "We had an assembly and they honored the scholarship recipients. When they called my name to come to the stage, I was worried. You know. School for us is a privilege, not a right. You and Mama drummed that into me before I went to an American school. But I felt different after everyone clapped. They clapped for me just like everybody else who got a scholarship."

"Did announcing your scholarship make things worse?" Papa asked.

"No, the opposite," Artemesia replied. "Jimmy Trouckman's girlfriend, Bea, invited me to a party at Jimmy's house. And, Jimmy said when I come to the party Mr. Trouckman will talk to me about helping you get your green card back."

Papa had been looking out toward the vineyard, with Artemesia in his peripheral vision. Now, his head whipped toward Artemesia and his eyes widened.

"What?" he said. "That doesn't seem possible. Mr. Trouckman has been angry with me since I began working for Mr. Markilsen and refused to work at his camp."

"I was pretty surprised," Artemesia said. "Bea also told me the kids from the Trouckman migrant camp are coming to the party and I can invite them to our English classes. But Bea and Jimmy and his friends have gone to school with me ever since we moved here, and I don't trust them.

"Do you have any specific reason not to trust them?" Papa asked.

"More of a general one," Artemesia replied.

"They've been clear that to them, migrants are a lower species of humans."

"Derogatory comments?" Papa asked.

"Yes," Artemesia said. "I've never made an effort to talk to them. Bea told me that my scholarship changed their opinion of me. But I don't know if I believe her."

"It's a nice thought, but sometimes strong opinions have thick roots," Papa said. "A while back you saw Mr. Trouckman arguing with Mr. Markilsen when you came home from school. He was the big man with the truck. Do you remember?"

"Yes, but I never saw his face," Artemesia said. "I remember he was angry about you hiring the families from his camp."

"Even before that, he disapproved of me," Papa said.

"I knew that, Mr. Markilsen told me," Artemesia

said. "Because of you, our vineyard is more profitable then the Trouckmans' because our grapes get to market first, and they never have enough workers to pick all their grapes before they spoil. But if Mr. Trouckman wants to help get your green card back and allows Jimmy to invite their migrant kids to the party, maybe he's changing."

"Do you believe that, or is it wishful thinking?" Papa asked.

"I'm wishing I believed it," Artemesia said. "It's like trying to look through someone's else's eyes. At school, after we finish a book, Mrs. Fisher holds team debates from the literary characters' points of view. We aren't allowed to disagree with our character's point of view. Instead, we must justify and explain our position based on the character's personal biases."

"So, from Bea's point of view, why did she invite Artemesia to Jimmy's party?" Papa asked.

"Because Bea thinks she's Jimmy's girlfriend and does everything he tells her to do," Artemesia said. "What I can't figure out is why Jimmy would invite me."

"Do you think any of them would physically harm you?" Papa asked, scowling.

"No," Artemesia said. "They're bullies without teeth. I've never gone anywhere that I didn't think was safe. You taught me that. Jimmy doesn't go anywhere without his group of friends. And Lloyd and Janet are his friends, but they aren't mean. Danny and Bea have said mean things about me at school, but I think it's mostly to impress Jimmy."

"I know you're worried that I don't have a green card anymore," Papa said. "But I don't think you should go to the party for me. If Trouckman was serious about my green card he could speak to me directly, or Mr. Markilsen."

"I didn't believe them about helping to get back your green card, either," Artemesia said. "But when I told Jimmy I wanted to invite their migrant kids to our English classes, he said he'd check with his father. So, maybe it's possible the Trouckmans are seeing us differently. He might regret that his attitude toward you encouraged Jerry Blankden to set you up to lose your green card."

"That's a hopeful view," Papa said. "It seems to me that whether or not Mr. Trouckman talks to you about my green card, or Jimmy invites the migrant kids from their camp, the people at the party will be the same kids you see at school."

"I hadn't thought of it that way," Artemesia said.

"Are you going to go?" Papa asked.

"I thought I needed your permission."

"Not for a long time, Artemesia," Papa said. "The young woman I wrote about can decide for herself. If you become uncomfortable, call me. Mr. Markilsen will let me use his station wagon and I'll come get you."

Artemesia couldn't resist the opportunity to try to get Papa's green card back. She had to attend the party. She didn't trust them, but she couldn't allow her herself to not believe them.

***

Everything about attending a party with these classmates she knew, but didn't know, and visiting the Trouckmans' home had left Artemesia feeling unsettled as Saturday arrived. *Bea said she'd bring an extra bathing suit. That's good. My cut-offs and tee-shirt are probably not their style. I've never even been in a real swimming pool.* She'd seen pools in magazines with voluptuous, nearly naked movie stars draping themselves over lawn furniture. When Artemesia pictured herself posing in one of the skimpy bathing suits, she felt her face flush at the thought of being so exposed.

Lloyd had borrowed his older brother's car and arrived at two o'clock with Janet sitting next to him. The car was only a two door, but Janet pulled her seat forward so Artemesia could climb in the back.

Other than "hello", and "nice to see you," Lloyd and Janet were quiet except for a few mumbled words to one another. They didn't smile and didn't quite frown. It was as if worry or sadness had invaded their thoughts. With their bodies slumped in their seats it was hard to believe they were going to a party. *Odd*, Artemesia thought. *Maybe that's their nature. Sort of depressed.*

"Is everything okay?" Artemesia asked.

Janet looked at Lloyd almost pleadingly. Lloyd

shook his head. "We're fine," Lloyd said. "Just some pressure from school, parents… the usual."

As they drove past the vineyards Artemesia realized that she knew exactly where they would turn off to the Trouckmans' property. It was the road by the bus stop where Jimmy and Danny caught the school bus. Just after Lloyd turned onto the road, a big sign appeared that read, TROUCKMAN VINEYARDS. Lloyd continued down the road to a paved area next to the circular driveway in front of the Trouckmans' house. *Wow, this is twice as big as Mr. Markilsen's house,* Artemesia thought.

"We're supposed to walk around to the back," Lloyd said. He took Janet's arm and Artemesia followed them. When they reached the pool area Janet placed her purse on a table near the sliding door by the back of the house. She gestured for Artemesia to do the same with her backpack.

Jimmy was lying on a lounge chair next to the pool. Bea was sitting by his feet, rubbing sunscreen onto his legs.

"Look who's arrived," Danny said. Artemesia hadn't seen him sitting under the sun umbrella until he spoke.

"Hello Arti," Jimmy said. "Danny, get Arti a drink and show her around, won't you, old man."

"Happy to old pal," Danny said. "Come on Arti, I'll fix you up and take you on the royal tour."

Uh-oh, Artemesia thought. *Danny sounds sloshed.* Sharon had warned her to be on the lookout for them sneaking alcohol into her drink. *But they weren't hiding it.* Danny took Artemesia's arm and led her toward the bar by the pool. The bottles were all marked, and nearly all were hard liquor.

"What's your poison, babe?" Danny asked.

"May I pour my own?" Artemesia asked.

"Good idea," he replied. "Steady hands. Make me another bourbon and seven while you're back there."

"Okay," Artemesia replied. "The bourbon is labeled. Tell me how much, and is *seven*, Seven-up?

"See that little metal cup," Danny said. "That's a jigger. Two of those and then Seven-up to the top of the glass."

"Got it," said Artemesia. She looked around the pool area. *No one except Jimmy and his thuggy friends.* She scolded herself. Sharon's term, *thuggy friends*, had amused her. *How easily the derogatory words slip in.*

"You should have one of these too," Danny said. "It'll ease your agony."

Agony? I wonder if he's talking about how he'll feel tomorrow. "I don't have your fortitude," Artemesia said. She found a bottle of tonic water and a bowl of cut limes. She poured herself a glass over ice and squeezed the lime piece before dropping it into her drink.

When she handed Danny his drink, he leaned on her and then staggered toward the back door.

"Come with me to the tour," he announced with an exaggerated sweep of his arm, nearly falling over.

"I saw that," Jimmy said. "Slow down on the booze, man. Bea, go help with the tour. Danny's useless."

"Sure Babe," Bea purred. She looked like the movie star Artemesia had imagined when she stood up. Slinky like. There was no way Bea could have gone swimming in the bathing suit she was wearing. Bea glided over to Artemesia and Danny, checking to make sure Jimmy was watching. He was.

"Is Arti your full name?" she asked.

"No," Artemesia is my full name."

"Come with me, Artemesia," she said. "Is that a family name?"

"No," Artemesia said. "It's the name of a spice flower. Is Bea short for Beatrice?"

"It is. Now aren't we cozy little friends."

Artemesia refused to hear her tone as meanness. *If I have any chance at getting Papa's green card back, I need to keep positive. I'm not used to her personality. She's trying to get to know me, and I need to try too.*

"I'm glad we're getting to know one another," Artemesia said. "I hope the bathing suit you brought for me covers up more. I don't have your figure." Artemesia knew Bea had failed two of her core classes. *Appearance is most important to her. Just as Jimmy needs to show off his father's wealth, she needs to show off her beauty.*

"No, I guess you don't have my figure," Bea said. "That's not your worry. It may be that no one will feel like swimming. Unless you want to swim by yourself."

"No," Artemesia said. "I wouldn't be comfortable being the only person in the swimming pool."

"Of course, you wouldn't," Bea said. "So, here we are in the back parlor, and then comes the formal dining room."

Artemesia watched the rooms go by as Bea led her. "When will the other kids get here?" Artemesia asked.

"By and by," Bea said.

I'm not sure what that means. "Where are Mr. and Mrs. Trouckman?" Artemesia asked.

"That question seemed to startle Bea. "Oh," Bea said. "They couldn't…. Well, not for a while…. Of course, Mr. Trouckman wants to talk to you about your father's green card. But I mean… First, they want to a…. show Jimmy they trust him to give a small pool party with his friends. And, here is Mr. Trouckman's study. Isn't it beautiful? You like to read, right? Check out his library. I need to use the bathroom. Wait here, I'll be right back."

There was a huge desk inlaid with leather toward one side of the room. In front were four high-back leather chairs spaced in an arc, facing the desk. Leather sofas were positioned on each side of the room, perpendicular to the desk, and a few feet away from the walls. Artemesia walked behind the furniture as she admired the woodworking detail in the paneled walls. Gruesome paintings, centered in the upper panels above the bookcases, loomed over her. A dog holding a bleeding rabbit in its teeth stood by an unpleasant looking man on a horse. Most of them were hunting scenes, except for one portrait. She wondered if the grim looking man was Mr. Trouckman. She had finished reading the spines of the books on two walls before Bea returned.

"That's enough tour," Bea said. "Back to the pool."

As they retraced their steps through the house Bea roused Danny from a chair in the dining room. "Come on, the party is just getting started."

Back outside, nothing had changed. Everyone was drinking. There was music, but no one was dancing. And no one was swimming. Bea and Jimmy started making out and Lloyd and Janet were still sitting together, their eyes downcast, with the same dour expressions they had when they picked her up. Danny was not quite unconscious, but close. He kept drinking.

Artemesia walked around the large patio, then she explored the manicured grounds that extended several hundred feet beyond the patio. She followed the patterned concrete paths that wound through ceramic planters, statues, and shrubs as she inspected the gardens. She looked for spices or eatables but found none. She noticed a distinct absence of insects.

No spiders or gnats or butterflies. She knew several of the flowered shrubs attracted moths and butterflies. *Poison. Probably good they don't grow food*, she thought.

It had been nearly two hours since the tour and nothing had changed, except now, Danny was snoring. She tried talking to the others and they answered her questions, but no one initiated a conversation. There was no sign of Mr. and Mrs. Trouckman or the migrants who lived at their camp. Before she had strong doubts about them, now she was nearly certain they had lied to her about helping with Papa's green card as well as other students and the migrants being invited.

She thought about weekends at home. The radio blaring, dancing outside, spicy cooking smells, chatter, laughter, piñatas hanging from the arbor's cross post, and blindfolding her sisters and Julio, then sending them off with the stick to beat out the candy. Papa's loud singing and counting while they tried to hide in the vineyard. The twins still hadn't figured out that all you do to find somebody is to follow their footprints in the soft dirt. Everything she cared about, everyone she loved was at home.

"Um, Lloyd, I'd like to go home now," Artemesia said. "Do you mind driving me?"

Lloyd's face clouded and tears sprung, clinging to his eyes. "You better ask Jimmy," Lloyd said.

Why, she wondered. Lloyd drove her here. *Strange custom. I'm not asking Jimmy's permission, but I'll tell him I'm leaving instead of just saying goodbye.*

"Jimmy, thank you for inviting me to your home," Artemesia said. "I'm glad that we have become better acquainted. I'm going home now."

"You can't leave," Jimmy said. "My father wants to speak with you about your father's green card. And, the kids from our migrant camp aren't here yet. Bea, you girls need to go swimming. We promised Arti. Take her into the pool house and give her a bathing suit. Bea, take your bag."

"I've been here for over two hours," Artemesia said. "Are your parents really going to come?"

"Of course," Jimmy said. "They'll be here soon."

Artemesia didn't believe him. *But why would he lie? What if Mr. Trouckman was delayed and did want to help Papa?* She studied Jimmy's expression without finding any clues.

"Let the games begin," Bea chirped. She unwrapped herself from Jimmy and picked up her bag. "Come on, Arti, and bring your backpack."

"Okay," Artemesia said.

"Are you coming Janet?" Bea asked.

"No," Janet said. "My stomach's upset. I don't feel like swimming."

Before Artemesia went inside the pool house, she saw Jimmy scowl at Janet. *More games*, she thought.

Another hour passed. Artemesia had swum laps and played with a beach ball after floating on a short board, while Bea sat on the highest pool step sipping her drink and barely touching the water.

Just about the time Artemesia had decided she'd waited long enough, a big man appeared from the back of the house. Artemesia knew immediately it was Mr. Trouckman and the scowl from the library portrait was his pleasant face. Now, his face was bright red, and he was screaming so loud she couldn't decipher his words. The noise roused Danny from his stupor, but Jimmy and Bea didn't look upset at all. Lloyd and Janet's faces darkened and twisted, and they were hunching over, as if they both might throw up.

"Police are coming..." Mr. Trouckman's words

started to make sense. "A thief in my home. My wallet... it was in my study, on my desk." His screaming had turned into bellowing. Mr. Trouckman stopped bellowing and looked around the pool area. His grim focus stopped on Artemesia. He nodded abruptly toward Jimmy and went back inside the house. Jimmy nodded toward Bea and followed his father.

Artemesia climbed the steps out of the water and retrieved a towel from the stack in front of the pool house. She decided not to change her clothes yet. She walked over to Lloyd and Janet. They looked even more upset than before.

"Should we go inside and help Mr. Trouckman look for his wallet?" Artemesia asked.

Lloyd gasped. Janet's eyes teared and she covered her face with her hands, then regained herself. "No," Lloyd said. "We are expected to stay right here."

Expected! What! "I'm going to change my clothes and call my father."

In the pool house dressing room Artemesia had taken off the wet bathing suit, toweled herself dry and finished dressing except for her shirt, which she had just begun to button when Mr. Trouckman, a policeman, and Jimmy burst through the door. She grabbed the damp towel and pressed it in front of her body. "Why are you here!" she demanded. "I'm dressing."

"Search her," Mr. Trouckman demanded. "My son generously extended an invitation to a migrant worker's daughter. I know her father. It's no surprise she's a thief."

"Mr. Trouckman," Artemesia said, "I didn't steal your wallet. I would never do such a thing. And my father is an honest man."

"Honest! He's an illegal. We'll see about you,"

Jimmy said. He was puffed up and held his lips in a cruel curl. Grabbing Artemesia's backpack, he unzipped both sides to the bottom. A black wallet with CDT embossed in the leather spilled out along with Artemesia's cloth wallet, breath mints and her tiny notebook with a short pencil attached.

"There, see!" Jimmy said. "She's the thief, and here's the proof!" He picked up the black leather wallet and handed it to the policeman.

"Is this your wallet, sir?" the policeman asked.

"Why yes, yes, it is," Mr. Trouckman said. "With my initials, Clarence David Trouckman. Now get this dirty Mexican out of my home. He jerked the towel away from Artemesia and threw it to the floor. "We'll need to burn that." He put his hand on Jimmy's shoulder and began a slow, purposeful walk out of the pool house. "Well son," he said, louder than necessary, "let this be a lesson to you about the importance of keeping a proper distance from the migrant workers."

Artemesia felt undressed standing in front of the policeman, even though he had looked aside. She quickly buttoned her shirt and slid her feet into her sandals. When the policeman finally turned toward Artemesia, he had a strange look on his face. Then he looked back in the direction Mr. Trouckman and Jimmy had taken.

Something about the policeman's expression restarted Artemesia's mind. *I see...finally. Now this all makes sense. I was the only guest and this whole thing was staged. Mr. Trouckman's angry words weren't sincere. This was like a play they wrote and acted out.*

"Come with me," the policeman said. "I'm Officer Nolan. You behave yourself and I won't cuff you, okay?"

"Okay," Artemesia said.

She followed the policeman out of the pool house. Mr. Trouckman and Jimmy stood stiffly in front of the back door. Danny and Bea had moved closer to the back door and were sitting on a bench, watching her. Artemesia wasn't surprised to see the smirks on their faces as she and Officer Nolan walked toward the parking area. Only Lloyd and Janet looked uncomfortable, their faces turned down as if they were unable to meet Artemesia's eye.

Officer Nolan held the back door of his police car open and Artemesia climbed inside. After they pulled out of the parking area, she looked through the metal grill separating her from Office Nolan and saw him watching her in the mirror.

"Young lady," he said, "how old are you?"

"Seventeen, sir," Artemesia answered.

"Where do you live?"

"At the Markilsen migrant camp. My father is the foreman."

"Have you been friends very long with the kids at the Trouckman's house?"

"No sir," Artemesia said. "It was a big surprise they invited me."

"Why did you go?" Officer Nolan asked.

Artemesia couldn't tell a policeman she went to the party get Papa's green card back. That would only add new problems.

"At our high school assembly, the principal introduced the students who received college scholarships," Artemesia said. "I was one of the students he introduced. He said he hoped we would inspire other students. I thought it inspired them to get to know me better. And, they promised to invite the kids from their migrant camp if I would come. But, now, I guess they just invited me to get me into trouble."

"Could be," Officer Nolan said.

Artemesia felt sick. Jimmy's sometimes girlfriend, Bea, leaving her in Mr. Trouckman's study for such a long time. The wallet in her backpack. Mr. Trouckman grabbing the towel from her. She shivered and put her head down. *I need to be satisfied with this life… forget about college. Maybe I won't even graduate from high school now.* She was too sad to cry. The weight of her heart forced her farther down on the police car's vinyl bench.

Artemesia's memories stirred as she watched the dust swirl between the grape vines from little gusts of wind. She thought of her mother. *Spice. Cooking spices… that's how she smelled.* She used to cook for the workers in the field. Artemesia imagined her mother's fingers, stained with ancho and carrots, caressing her cheek. *My sweet Artemesia flower,* Mama had called her. The heat in the police car stole her tiny tear before it could fall.

Even before she attended school, Mama and Papa told her she would be the first in their family to attend college. They didn't understand about being a migrant outside of the camp. But Artemesia did, and so did Haidee, Maria, Julio and Lucinda. She had prepared her sisters and brother for the name calling and nasty tricks from the other kids.

There were so many things that hadn't turned out the way she'd thought they would. Four years ago, when she was thirteen, Mr. Markilsen promoted Papa to foreman. They would live at the camp all year and attend local schools. She had never thought living in the United States for the whole year would be possible. One year after that, Mama decided to go to Mexico and bring Grandma to live with them. Only, they never came. Papa wrote letters, called people he knew, and even went to Mexico to find them, but no one knew what happened.

The dusty leaves hiding the grapes alongside the road reminded Artemesia of the coming harvest. It was a good year for the Markilsen vineyard. The sweet plump grapes underneath the leaves were almost ready. The seedless concords would sell for the best price. The grenaches and semillons would be picked, crushed, and sold to wineries. The rest of the grapes would be picked from their stems, laid between burlap layers below their vines, and dried. Specialty raisins took the most work and this year every house at their camp was filled with workers.

Remembering Mr. Trouckman's yelling about the families Papa hired from the Trouckman camp forced Artemesia back to the present.

"Officer Nolan, may I call my father?"

"Yes, but first we'll stop at the main jail for

paperwork," he replied. "When that's done, I'll take you to juvenile hall. You can call your parents from there."

Artemesia didn't complain. Growing up in the in the fields with her parents had taught her to follow the rules. If there was fourteen hours of sun, they worked fourteen hours. In the valley, the days ranged from nine hours of sun to fourteen in July. Ten years, they had worked for Mr. Markilsen. Even before Papa became the all-year foreman, they had stayed long past harvest, each family member doing what was needed.

Officer Nolan drove up to a closed overhead door and pressed the intercom. "Single female juvenile for booking," he said. After the overhead door rose to its highest position and stopped, he drove inside. There were three bays, like McDonald's drive-up windows, but each one had a parking space. Officer Nolan drove forward and parked next to the last window.

He didn't say anything or even look at Artemesia. He just got out, opened her door, then turned and walked through a small door next to the window. Artemesia followed him.

The woman at the desk inside frowned. "You know you're supposed to handcuff them before you bring them inside," she said.

"She's a kid," Officer Nolan said. "The only reason I didn't cite and release her is because Trouckman's on the warpath. Doesn't like her family for some reason."

"Oh, you do have a problem," the woman said, looking at Artemesia. "Trouckman dumped a lot of money into the Sheriff's election and thinks everyone in law enforcement works for him." The woman walked to a unit of open cubbyholes and began pulling forms out and putting them back. "Darn," she said.

"John, I'm all out of fingerprint cards, I'll be right back."

"Okay," Officer Nolan said. "We'll be right here."

After she left, he turned to Artemesia. "Do you know why Trouckman doesn't like your family?" he asked.

"I think so," Artemesia replied. She told him about the day Mr. Trouckman came to their camp and yelled at Papa and Mr. Markilsen about hiring the seven migrant families.

"So Trouckman's not too fond of Markilsen either?" Officer Nolan said.

"He didn't seem to be," Artemesia said. "But Mr. Trouckman knew his workers were leaving. They told him."

"I still don't understand why you went to a party at the Trouckman house," he said.

"I shouldn't have," Artemesia said.

The woman came back and pressed each of Artemesia's fingers into a light ink and then onto a card with ten boxes. "John," she said, "We shouldn't let Trouckman push us around. Why don't you call Judge Sanderson out at Juvenile Hall and see if she'll let you release Ms. Garcia to her father? You could interview her father when you take her home."

"Good idea, Cheryl," Officer Nolan said. He walked into an adjoining room and closed the door.

When he returned, Cheryl asked, "What did the Judge say?"

"She agreed to let me take her home."

***

From the back of the police car, Artemesia saw Papa turn off the radio and Haidee signal for the younger ones to follow her inside. The door was closed with

Papa standing in front of the house when Officer Nolan parked.

"Mr. Garcia," Officer Nolan said. "The Trouckmans have made a complaint against your daughter."

Papa looked at Artemesia. "Artemesia, are you hurt?"

"No, Papa," she said. "But, maybe it's worse."

Papa held out his arms for her and she rushed in. *Oh, this feels so good. So safe.* Papa led them to the outside table with benches. As the two men sat down, Artemesia looked at them and hesitated. *Should I leave… No, this is about me. I'm staying.* She sat down on the bench on the same side as her father, but not too close. Papa looked at her and nodded.

"Good," he said. "I'm glad you stayed, Artemesia. Whatever happened, we have better solutions when we all work on the problem."

"Haidee," Papa called. "Bring three glasses and a pitcher of limeade with ice for us."

"Okay Papa," Haidee called from inside the house. Artemesia knew her sisters and brother would be sitting by the closest wall, listening.

As Artemesia explained what had happened at the Trouckman house, the muscles in Papa's face drew together in tight lines against his angular bones. Artemesia saw him struggle to hold back a storm cloud of anger as she revealed the long history of demeaning behaviors Jimmy and his friends had shown toward her at school.

"My daughter is not a thief," Papa said. "Trouckman is angry with me. My daughter only went to the party to get my green card back."

Artemesia gasped, "Papa, no!"

Officer Nolan looked puzzled for a moment and

then he raised his eyes to Papa. "Sir, your immigration status is not why I'm here."

"It doesn't matter," Papa said. "My daughter is not a criminal. Even though they promised to invite the kids from their migrant camp, and she hoped to invite them to her English classes, she wouldn't have gone unless she thought it could help get my green card back."

"Papa…." Artemesia said.

"No, Artemesia," Papa interrupted. "I didn't realize how badly you've been treated by Jimmy Trouckman's crowd for all these years. But I do know you pretended that the other reasons for attending the party were just as important to you as helping me get back my green card. They weren't."

"Is that true, Artemesia?" Officer Nolan asked.

"Yes, I… suppose," Artemesia responded. "But,

if the police know my father is here illegally, he will be deported."

"The police department is not the same agency as immigration, but…" Officer Nolan looked at Papa for a moment while he hesitated. Then he looked back at Artemesia. "It's true that your father's status might leak from my report to other agencies. But, if the Judge knew the real reason you went to the party, it might help your defense against the criminal charge. Artemesia, you should decide. I won't write any information about your father's green card in the report, if that's what you want."

"Yes," Artemesia said, "That's what I want."

Artemesia looked straight into her father's eyes, almost like a challenge. His storm cloud expression softened, and he nodded briefly, putting his hand over hers on the table.

"I'll need information about the other reasons you

attended the party. Did anyone else hear Bea tell you Trouckman's migrant kids were coming to the party?"

"We were on the bus," Artemesia said. "Bea. She sat with me, and …"

Suddenly, the door burst open and Haidee, followed by Julio, Maria and Lucinda, rushed toward them. "I heard," Maria said. "Me too," Lucinda said. "We all heard," Haidee said.

Artemesia watched Officer Nolan's mouth turn down with effort as he tamed his smile.

"Okay, one at a time," he said. He was holding his notebook and used his pen to point to Haidee. "Tell me your name."

"Haidee Eva Garcia," she said. "We were sitting at the back of the bus, in the long row. Artemesia sat in the middle of the bus, which is as far back as the high school kids are allowed. Bea was practically shouting, like she wanted everyone to hear. They usually whisper, but when we saw Bea sit with Artemesia, we were all amazed."

"Why?" Officer Nolan asked.

"Because we're migrant kids," Julio said. "They don't sit with us."

"I'm going to have trouble keeping track of what each of you tell me. Let's start with me writing down all your names," Officer Nolan said. When he finished, he said, "Let's start with you, Lucinda. Did you hear Bea invite your sister to a party?"

"Yes," Lucinda said. "Artemesia was as surprised as me. She didn't say anything for a little while."

"Did Bea say who else was invited to the party?" Officer Nolan asked.

"Kids from the high school were invited and migrant kids from Mr. Trouckman's camp," Lucinda said.

"You're sure that Bea said other migrant kids were invited?" Officer Nolan asked.

"I'm sure," Lucinda said. "And all of us heard her say that. We even had a family discussion about it. Artemesia decided to go to the party because of Papa's green card and she wanted to invite the migrant kids to our English class."

"Were you all at the family discussion?" Officer Nolan asked.

"No," Lucinda said. "Papa and Artemesia talked about it, we just listened at the wall. Like we did today."

This time Officer Nolan didn't hold back his grin.

"Thank you, Lucinda," he said. "Does anybody have anything else to tell me about Bea and Jimmy and the other kids inviting Artemesia to the party?"

"Julio looked at Haidee and said, "Artemesia wouldn't steal anything. We should tell him that?

Haidee, Maria and Lucinda looked at Julio, then each other, before Haidee spoke, "We told you everything that we saw on the bus when Artemesia was invited. But, Julio's right. We all know Artemesia would never steal."

Everyone looked at Officer Nolan as if they had asked him a question.

"Okay," he said. "Good character opinions don't help much in court. The way we can help Artemesia is by gathering facts about what happened that can be proven in court. I'll need to get the names of other students that ride the bus who might have overheard Bea tell Artemesia the migrant kids were invited. Then I'll talk to a few more people and write my report. Artemesia, Mr. Garcia, kids, I'll let you know what happens next, when I know." he said.

Papa's face was still tight as they watched Officer Nolan drive away. Once the dust from the police car settled, Papa set his jaw in determination and looked at his children.

"That's all we can do for now," Papa said. "Julio, start the pit fire. There's a piece of goat meat in the refrigerator. Maria, bring it out with the roasting pan and we'll have it for supper. Lucinda, you pick a music station, so we can dance."

Lucinda chose a Mariachi station and as soon as the music started Artemesia felt better. She circled Lucinda, matching her three side steps, then a shimmy down and up to the trumpet's rhythm. Still dancing, they headed inside to chop the salad vegetables. Haidee cut more limes and when Maria returned from placing the covered goat roast onto the fire brick, they shimmied and bumped hips while they made more limeade and mixed the flour with the lard for tortillas. Dust puffed up with Papa's and Julio's stomps in the soft dirt as they clapped to the

Mariachi beat in between heating the refried beans and tending the fire.

"Eee yai eee," Julio called with the music as Papa spun him around. Julio laughed, then shouted, "We have everything!"

Papa's determination to change the mood only helped Artemesia through dinner. After that, her emotions spun between fury, agony and humiliation. *I can't believe how stupid I was. Come to the party... we'll let the other migrants in to keep you company. You like to read.... Isn't this a beautiful library? ... And Jimmy's father.... Ripping away the towel. I hate them all. No... then I'm like them... hateful.*

Monday, Artemesia steeled herself for school as she followed Haidee, Julio, Maria and Lucinda into the bus. Bea and Danny were sitting together. Janet was sitting alone in the seat in front of Artemesia's. *What's up with this? Bea and Janet always sit together until Lloyd gets on the bus.* None of them looked at her. *Two more stops.... That's when Jimmy and Lloyd get on. I hope they don't look at me either.*

"Well, well, there's the little thief!" Jimmy crowed as he stepped into the bus. "Already out of the slammer?"

"I am not a thief," Artemesia said. "You set me up. Your actions are despicable."

"Oh, poor little Artemesia," Bea said. "You want to sit by me in assembly, now that we're such good friends?"

"Never," said Artemesia. She glanced back at her sisters and brother. They smiled, and Haidee gave her a thumbs-up.

Lloyd sat with Janet in front of her. Janet leaned her head close to him.

"It's wrong… we should tell," Janet whispered.

"No," Lloyd whispered. "We can't. My dad will lose his job."

This is a new trick…., Artemesia thought. *Or maybe an old one…. Acting sad…. Pretending they were forced to participate. Pretending they're not part of the thuggy friend group… Even if it's true, they should have warned me. They picked me up.*

***

Wednesday, after school, the telephone rang.

"Hello," Artemesia said.

"Hello, this is Officer Nolan. May I speak with Mr. Garcia?"

Ache gripped Artemesia's heart. She could barely breathe, as if the air was stuck in her throat.

"Hello," Officer Nolan said. "Are you still there?"

Artemesia straightened her body and forced herself to respond.

"Yes. This is Artemesia, Officer Nolan. My father is working. Should I have him call you?"

"Could you ask him to meet me at your house tomorrow at four o'clock?"

"All right, tomorrow then. I'll tell him."

***

Artemesia stood with Papa and watched Officer Nolan park his police car. Haidee, Julio, Maria and Lucinda were inside the house and the limeade and glasses were outside on the table. After Officer Nolan shook Papa's hand, he reached out toward Artemesia. She studied his hand, momentarily confused, then grasped his hand with hers. He smiled.

"I interviewed the other kids that ride the bus with you, Artemesia," Officer Nolan said. "And some of your classmates and teachers. Two other kids remembered Bea telling you that the Trouckman migrant kids were coming to the party. Several people overheard Jimmy Trouckman make disparaging remarks about migrant kids, particularly you. And your teachers all expressed disbelief that you would have committed this theft against Mr. Trouckman, or anyone."

Officer Nolan looked at Papa and said, "When I spoke with Mr. Trouckman, he didn't try to hide his dislike for you, Mr. Garcia, nor his poor attitude toward migrant workers in general. The Trouckmans and Jimmy's friends all deny that other migrants were invited. But you folks have a good reputation. I interviewed Mr. Markilsen, and he spoke highly of your whole family."

"It sure looks like this whole wallet theft scenario was made up by Jimmy and his friends to cause Artemesia problems. My watch commander agreed that Artemesia was set up. Trouckman refused to consider whether his son was involved and insisted we send the investigation report to the District Attorney's Office, which we did. Initially, they agreed that charges against Artemesia were not warranted."

"Initially?" Papa asked.

"Apparently, Trouckman gave money for the district attorney's re-election and now, he's called in a favor."

"What's going to happen?" Artemesia asked.

"The District Attorney's Office will probably file charges against you in Juvenile Court," Officer Nolan said. "When they do, you will be sent an order to appear in court."

"Will there be a trial?" Papa asked.

"I doubt that Trouckman will drop this. So, yes, I think there will be a trial," Officer Nolan answered. "I'll be there, Artemesia. I'll testify on your behalf. I've been a cop for eighteen years. No one at the

Trouckman house behaved as if this was a real theft, even Mr. Trouckman. He didn't even try to check inside his wallet after his boy took it from your back-pack. I'll tell that to the judge."

**

The order to appear arrived a week later and ten days after that Papa borrowed Mr. Markilsen's station wagon. The whole family came to Juvenile Court. They arrived an hour early so Artemesia could meet with her court-appointed lawyer.

"Hello, Artemesia," the lawyer said. "I'm Jennifer Buckley."

Papa, Haidee, Julio, Maria and Lucinda were all sitting on the bench in the hallway. The lawyer shook hands with everyone, asking their names.

"Artemesia and I are going to speak privately for a moment," she said.

***

When Artemesia and the lawyer returned, the bailiff announced in the hallway that Artemesia's case was next. As they rounded the hallway corner, Artemesia saw Mr. Trouckman and Jimmy pushing open the courtroom door.

Artemesia gasped.

"What's wrong, Artemesia," the lawyer asked.

"That's Mr. Trouckman and his son, Jimmy," she said.

"They shouldn't be here," the lawyer said. "Keep your head up and walk into the courtroom with me."

The lawyer gestured for Artemesia's family to sit in the front row. Mr. Trouckman and Jimmy were standing on the other side talking to the man in front of a low barrier.

"All stand," the bailiff said, "The Court shall come to order, the Honorable Judge Sanderson, presiding."

"Be seated," the judge said, as soon as she sat down. "This is the Matter of Artemesia Garcia. Who are all these people in my courtroom?"

Artemesia's lawyer stood up immediately. "Good morning, your Honor. Next to me is Artemesia Garcia and behind me is her father, Bonifacio Garcia and her siblings, Haidee, Julio, Maria and Lucinda. I request the Court's permission for Miss Garcia's family to attend these proceedings."

"Is this your wish, Miss, Garcia?" the judge asked.

"Yes, ma'am," Artemesia said.

"Very well, permission granted," the judge said. "Now, who are these other people?"

"This is the complaining witness and his son," the deputy district attorney said. "I request permission for them to attend."

"This is juvenile court and you're a prosecutor. You know better, Mr. Evans," Judge Sanderson said.

"Unless, of course, Miss Garcia consents to them staying." The judge looked at Artemesia and said, "Miss Garcia, do you want these people in the courtroom?"

"No, ma'am," Artemesia answered.

"She appears to have better sense than you, Mr. Evans," the judge said. "Bailiff, please escort these men out."

"Glad to see you, Garcia," Mr. Trouckman said, as he walked past Papa.

After discussing dates with the lawyers, the judge said, "Trial will be scheduled in three weeks." She stood up and left the courtroom. The bailiff wrote down the trial date and handed the paper to Papa.

***

For the day of the trial, Papa had arranged for everyone to miss school. Artemesia felt helpless. She knew Jimmy and his friends would lie. Mr. Johnston said he would bring Artemesia's school records, including Papa's scholarship letter. *But how could that help?*

When they arrived at the courthouse, Artemesia's lawyer was waiting for them in the hallway. "Artemesia, do you know Janet Stewart and Lloyd Decker?" she asked.

"Yes, I go to school with them. They're friends of Jimmy Trouckman," Artemesia said.

"They're in the next room with Lloyd's father. They told me that Jimmy Trouckman and his father, together, falsified evidence of the wallet theft. Lloyd and Janet believed that Lloyd's father would be fired from his accounting firm if they didn't go along with the plan. When Lloyd finally told his father, his father told his employer what had happened. The partners at his accounting firm decided they didn't need Mr. Trouckman as a client."

The bailiff's voice carried down the hallway, "The Matter of Artemesia G. is being called."

When they reached the door, Mr. Trouckman and Jimmy were trying to push past the bailiff. "Move aside," Mr. Trouckman said.

"You're not on my list. Wait in the hallway," the bailiff said.

The bailiff held the door open as Artemesia's lawyer led Artemesia and her family past the Trouckmans.

"Are there any additions to the witness lists?" the judge asked.

"Yes, your Honor," Artemesia's lawyer said. "Janet Stewart and Lloyd Decker are added to the minor's witnesses.

"I object," the deputy district attorney said.

"Why?" asked the judge.

"We have had no notice. I haven't been provided with witness statements."

"I guess we'll just have to hear the evidence from the witness stand," the judge said. "Let's get started. Mr. Evans call your first witness."

Mr. Evans went out the door to the hallway. He was gone for several minutes and came back with Mr. Trouckman and Jimmy. "Uh, your Honor, there's been a development. I… uh … request an opportunity to interview these surprise witnesses prior to trial."

"Are you asking for a continuance?" The judge asked.

Artemesia heard Mr. Trouckman's loud whisper to Jimmy, "Go outside and call them. Tell them to hurry up." Jimmy scurried out of the courtroom.

"No, no, not at all, your Honor, I don't want a continuance," the deputy district attorney said. "I just need a little time to talk with these witnesses."

"Why do I have the feeling you're playing a game?"

the judge asked. "Mr. Evans, do you know these witnesses' relationship to the case?"

"Well... um, yes, your Honor. But I wish to explore some specifics before they take the witness stand."

"That's what cross-examination is for," the judge said. "Put your case on and talk to them at the break. Both attorneys assured me that this trial will be completed in one day. Let's get going."

Jimmy returned followed by two men in black jackets with Immigration patches on the front and the agency initials in large letters on the back.

"What's going on?" the judge said. "Bailiff, remove these people from my courtroom!"

"Hold on, Judge," one of the Immigration men said. He held up a piece of paper. "I have an arrest warrant for Bonifacio Garcia. I have reliable information that he is sitting right there." He pointed to Papa.

"Bailiff bring me the warrant," the judge said. As she read it, her face sagged as her body slumped down in her chair. "Yes, this is a legal warrant from a federal magistrate. Mr. Garcia, there is nothing I can do. I am so sorry. You will need to go with these men."

The men stepped into the aisle, pulled Papa up, and handcuffed him. Mr. Trouckman stood and walked toward them. "Thanks for taking out the trash, boys," he said. He put one hand on Jimmy's shoulder and gestured with the other toward the Garcia children, "I don't care about the rest of 'em. Let's go Jimmy." They left the courtroom.

Papa forced the men to stop as he turned around. Artemesia stood by the table and Haidee, Julio, Maria and Lucinda stood in the front row. The immigration men's faces were tilted up, lit with pride and arrogance. For one moment, Papa's eyes held his family. No one seemed to breathe as the immigration men pushed Papa out of the courtroom, and the door closed.

The End.